UNCLE PIRATE

to the rescue

Also by Douglas Rees
UNCLE PIRATE

Uncle Pirate

to the
RESCUE

by Douglas Rees • illustrations by Tony Auth

Factory

Hyena of
the Seas

Message in
a Bottle

The Big Island

Margaret K. McElderry Books
New York London Toronto Sydney

MARGARET K. McELDERRY BOOKS

An imprint of Simon & Schuster Children's Publishing Division
1230 Avenue of the Americas, New York, New York 10020

This book is a work of fiction. Any references to historical events, real people, or real locales are used fictitiously. Other names, characters, places, and incidents are products of the author's imagination, and any resemblance to actual events or locales or persons, living or dead, is entirely coincidental.

MARGARET K. McELDERRY BOOKS is a trademark of Simon and Schuster, Inc.

For information about special discounts for bulk purchases, please contact Simon & Schuster Special Sales at 1-866-506-1949 or business@simonandschuster.com.

The Simon & Schuster Speakers Bureau can bring authors to your live event. For more information or to book an event, contact the Simon & Schuster Speakers Bureau at 1-866-248-3049 or visit our website at www.simonspeakers.com.

Book design by Lauren Rille
The text for this book is set in Edlund.
The illustrations for this book are rendered in pencil with pen and ink on paper.
Manufactured in the United States of America
0310 OFF
2 4 6 8 10 9 7 5 3 1
Library of Congress Cataloging-in-Publication Data
Rees, Douglas.
Uncle Pirate to the rescue / Douglas Rees ; illustrated by Tony Auth.—1st ed.
p. cm.
Summary: When Captain Desperate Evil Wicked Bob receives a plea from his former crew, he heads out to rescue them and is soon followed by his nephew Wilson, Commodore Purvis, Captain Jack, and others who fear that he needs to be rescued as well.
ISBN 978-1-4169-7505-2 (pbk. : alk. paper)
ISBN 978-1-4169-9916-4 (eBook)
[1. Pirates—Fiction. 2. Rescues—Fiction. 3. Uncles—Fiction. 4. Penguins—Fiction. 5. Schools—Fiction. 6. Humorous stories.] I. Auth, Tony, ill. II. Title.
PZ7.R25475Unh 2010
[Fic]—dc22
2009009130

FIRST
EDITION

For Phil, Des, and Dillon. Shipmates.
—D. R.

For Katie and Emily, as they begin their voyages

—T. A.

Ship's Articles
Writ by Captain Desperate Evil Wicked Bob
Sign or Go Ashore Like a Lubber.

1) We be the crew of the good ship <u>Kraken.</u> We swears to stand together in all storms, battles, and other pirate dangers.

2) We swears to follow all lawful orders shipshape and Bristol fashion.

3) We also swears never to mutiny.

4) Captain Desperate Evil Wicked Bob swears never to hang, shoot, or keelhaul any member of the crew.

5) Except for mutiny.

6) All treasure is to be divided up even.

7) We be the crew of the good ship <u>Kraken.</u> We swears to stand together in all storms, battles, and other pirate dangers. We swears it again.

8) Captain Desperate Evil Wicked Bob swears to bring Captain Jack to school every day. Unless the bird be sick.

These be the articles signed by every sea dog at Jolly Roger Elementary School, that used to be Very Elementary School until Capt. Desperate Evil Wicked Bob took it over.

UNCLE  PIRATE

to the rescue

BAD NEWS BOTTLE

I found the message in the mailbox when I got home from school. It was in an old thunder-slump bottle that was covered with sand and barnacles and had a cork. Inside was a letter. If you looked hard through the blue glass, you could see that it said:

TO CAPTIN DESPRIT EVEL WIKED BOB
PLESE DILEVER
WE PAYZ IN GOLD

On the outside of the bottle was a note from the mailman. It said, "I guess this is yours. If it is, you owe me $14.35. Gold will be fine, but ordinary money is too. Your Postal Carrier."

Uncle Pirate never got mail. I could hardly wait for him and Captain Jack to get home from school so he could open it.

I took it in to show to my mother.

"Look at this," I said. "A note in a bottle for Uncle Pirate. That's exciting."

"Exciting? Maybe," Mom said, and looked worried. "But I've got a bad feeling about it. I think I'd better start making a pumpkin pie."

"Uh-oh," I said.

My mom makes the best pumpkin pie in the world. But Dad and I call it Bad News Pie, because she only makes it when she has bad news. Now she was making it before she even knew what the news was. That scared me.

It was hard to wait for my uncle and his penguin to get home.

Uncle Pirate had to work extra hours every day because he ran the school. Ms. Quern helped him with all the paperwork. She was the school secretary. She was also Uncle Pirate's sweetheart. He called her Ferocious Lovely Eunice.

Captain Jack the penguin always stayed late to study with his friend Long Carla. The more she taught him, the more she knew. They were both getting pretty smart.

We had a principal, Mr. Purvis. But everyone knew Uncle Pirate was our real commander. Principal Purvis loved having Uncle Pirate around, because now he didn't have to do any work. He loved the pirate name Uncle Pirate had given him, which was Sneaky Purvis. He loved his new rank, which was commodore. He'd stopped wearing suits to school and started wearing a white uniform with lots of gold braid. We all saluted him on the playground. It made him very happy.

We've all been happy since Uncle Pirate and Captain Jack came to stay with us. Uncle Pirate had turned us all into pirates. Now we all had pirate names, and we ran our classrooms like ships. We all liked school and treated each other like shipmates. What would happen to us if he left? Would Jolly Roger Elementary go back to being the awful place it had been? Would we stop being pirates? Would I stop being Binnacle Will and go back to just being Wilson? Would Sand Crab Scott and Hammerhead Jason go back to breaking my glasses every week?

It was a terrible thought.

Finally, I saw Uncle Pirate, Captain Jack, and Ms. Quern slowly coming up the street to our house. Uncle Pirate always walked slowly because he only had one leg. Captain Jack walked slowly because he was a penguin. Ms. Quern walked slowly because she liked walking with them.

Ms. Quern turned off at her house, and Uncle Pirate and Captain Jack said good-bye to her.

I ran toward them.

"Uncle Pirate, you've got mail. It's in a bottle. Mom thinks it's bad news. It's not bad news, is it, Uncle Pirate?"

"Message in a bottle? Belike some mollymockery or other," Uncle Pirate said.

"Let me read it," said Captain Jack. "I'm good at reading."

"Ye be good at everything, Captain Jack," Uncle Pirate said. He gave the penguin a hug. "There be not another penguin between here and the South Pole knows as much as ye do. Ye be a rare bird, matey. Aye. Ye shall read the note to me."

We all sat down at the table in the kitchen. Mom handed Uncle Pirate the bottle. He opened it and pulled out the message.

"Here ye go, Captain Jack," he said.

"Nice big printing," Captain Jack said. "It starts, 'Dere Captin Desprit Evel Wiked Bob'— This is very bad spelling."

"Then belike it comes from a true pirate," Uncle Pirate said. "Go on."

This note be a kry four help. It be from yer old first mate Disgusting Earl. Plese do not stop reding it. I be riting to beg ye to reskew yer old crew. We be emprizind on a most tearable eyeland. I knows we treated ye bad, mahrooning ye

5

in Antartika and all. That were very rong
of us. We has no rite to ask fer yer
help. But we be in most desprit strates.
We apeels to yer brave and good nachure,
hopeing ye will fergive yer old shipmates
from the Hyena of the Seas and kum and
save us.

Best wishes,
Disgusting Earl
and fourty sorry old shipmates of yers.

Then came a whole line of *X*s. Forty of them.

"I can write a lot better than this," Captain Jack
said.

"Let me clap eyes on that paper," Uncle Pirate said.
"It be from Disgusting Earl, all right. I'd know his
crabby fist in a sea chest of homework."

Uncle Pirate sat staring at the message for a long
time. Mom, Captain Jack, and I sat staring at him.

Finally, Uncle Pirate said, "Me old crew needs me
help."

"But they don't even say where they are," I said.

"They won't be knowin' that," Uncle Pirate said.
"Trapped on an island be all they know." He shook his
head. "Pirates be a mess of chowderheads, mostly."

"I'd better check on my pie," Mom said. She was starting to cry.

"You're not going to try to find them, are you, Uncle Pirate?" I asked. "I mean, everyone needs you here. And like you said, you don't even know where they are."

"Well, *I'm* not going anywhere," Captain Jack said. "I've got too much homework."

Uncle Pirate didn't say anything. He just folded his arms and looked solemn.

He sat there until Dad came home.

"Arh, Bob," Dad said.

Uncle Pirate didn't say anything, so Dad said, "Arh?"

Uncle Pirate shook his head. Then he got up and went out to look at the sunset.

I went with him. We watched the sky turn dark. The first star came out.

"They be out there somewhere, Nevvy," he said. "Me old crew."

"We're your crew too," I said. "Those other guys marooned you."

"Arh," said Uncle Pirate. And that was all he said.

We had dinner, but I couldn't eat my Bad News Pie. I gave my piece to Uncle Pirate. He put it next to his own and pushed them together. He didn't eat a bite.

That night Uncle Pirate left. He waited until Mom and Dad were asleep and Captain Jack was curled up in his refrigerator. Then he sneaked down the stairs with his trunk on his back and his cutlass in his belt.

I know because I was standing on the porch, right in front of the door. When he opened it, I asked, "Who's going to run the school?"

Uncle Pirate said, "Walk with me a bit, Nevvy."

We went down the street together. Uncle Pirate limped along without saying anything until we came to a stoplight.

"Ye be right, Nevvy," he said. "I has a new crew now. And the school be my duty station. But I be right too. Old shipmates in need must be helped. Even if they be a bucket of no-good, low-down, mutinous shark bait." Then he said, "Nevvy, ye be the best shipmate I ever had. Better'n Captain Jack, even. I've left a letter. It be for . . ."

He couldn't talk because he had a lump in his throat.

"Ms. Quern," I said.

"Aye," Uncle Pirate said. "Tell her—"

The light changed and he crossed the street. I watched until I couldn't see him anymore.

But I could hear him singing,

"Oh the loneliest place
On the earth's lovely face
Is wherever ye long for yer sweetheart.
And the song of the sea
Though it's noble and free
Cannot comfort a most incomplete heart.
Oh, Secretary, oh, Secretary,
Oh, Secretary so dear,
Me heart broke on the day
That you wandered away
From our little shack down by the pier."

HYENA OF THE SKIES

I took Ms. Quern's letter to her at school. I took the note from the pirates, too. Commodore Purvis had me read it aloud in an assembly.

After Uncle Pirate had been gone a week, we got a postcard from Hawaii. On one side it said ALOHA in shiny letters. On the other side it said, "No sign of a sail yet. I makes for Tahiti."

After three weeks we got another postcard. It said TAHITI on one side. On the other it said, "Mayhap I has a sniff of 'em. Bearing south-southwest. Keep all Bristol fashion, Nevvy. I'll be back."

After that, we didn't get any more postcards.

I took each of the postcards to school as soon as they came. Commodore Purvis had more special assemblies and made me read them. The teachers did lessons on Hawaii and Tahiti. But it was all sad. We still called

each other by our pirate names, and we said Lafitte's Oath, along with the Pledge of Allegiance, but it wasn't the same without Uncle Pirate. If it hadn't been for Captain Jack, we'd all have gone back to fighting each other and frightening Commodore Purvis. But everybody knew Captain Jack needed a quiet place to learn, and nobody wanted him to stop coming to their classes. So we still behaved according to articles.

On the last day of school, I made a plan. That night I would sneak out of my house and go down to the bus depot. I would spend all of my money on a ticket to the Pacific Ocean. And if I didn't have enough money, I would ride as far as I could and walk the rest of the way. Because I was sure that Uncle Pirate was in trouble. And whatever kind of trouble it was, I was going to find him and bring him home.

That's what I was thinking about when Ms. Quern came into our room.

"Everybody down to the cafetorium," she said. "We're having an assembly."

All the kids in school were marching down the halls. The *Sea Dragon*s, the *Stingray*s, the *Hammerhead*s, the *Narwhal*s, the *Swordfish*es, the *Sea Lion*s, and my class, the *Kraken*s. When we were all sitting in the cafetorium, shipshape and Bristol fashion, Commodore Purvis turned off the lights and started a PowerPoint presentation.

"I know we're all worried about Captain Desperate Evil Wicked Bob," he said. "We're afraid he may be in trouble and need our help. Some of you may even be planning to run away from home to go look for him. So I've called this assembly to show you why you don't have to."

A picture of Uncle Pirate flashed on the screen.

"This is our missing captain," he said.

Flash.

"This is the note from his old crew," he said.

Flash.

"This is his last communication to us," he went on, "saying he's bearing south-southwest."

Flash.

"This is the southwest Pacific," he said.

A map that was all blue, with small black dots on it, came on the screen.

"Somewhere out here is where he is," Commodore Purvis said. "But how can we find him? That's the biggest ocean in the world."

Flash.

A picture of a boat came up next.

"This is how most people would go searching," Commodore Purvis went on. "Slow and old-fashioned. But that's not what I'm going to do."

Next came a picture of a big black airship floating over our town. On its side was a skull and crossbones.

"This is the *Hyena of the Skies*," Commodore Purvis

said. "It's an old US Navy blimp I got for a dollar. I've learned how to fly it, and I'm going to use the *Hyena* to find the captain. With this craft, I can scout thousands of miles of ocean in a day. I'll find Captain Desperate Evil Wicked Bob and bring him home. I should be back in a week. Maybe two."

"Who's going with you?" I asked.

"Nobody," Commodore Purvis said. "There's no room. Besides, I don't need any help. I want to have this adventure all to myself. I've never had an adventure before."

The lights came back on.

"So you can all enjoy your vacations. Just have a good time, and when I get back with our captain, I'll fly over the school so everyone can see we're home."

We all just sat there.

"If you want to clap, go ahead," Principal Purvis said.

No one did.

Long Carla raised her hand.

"That's a big blimp, Commodore. How come there's only room for you?"

"I had to put in extra fuel tanks," he said. "That's a lot of weight."

"Penguins are light," Captain Jack said.

Commodore Purvis acted like he hadn't heard him. "You're all excused," he said.

Captain Jack and I walked home together hand-in-flipper.

"Sneaky Purvis is up to something," Captain Jack said. "He can't rescue the captain. He's not smart enough. He's not brave enough, either."

"I know," I said, "but I don't care."

"Why not?" Captain Jack asked.

"Because whatever he's up to, I'm going with him."

"Me too," Captain Jack said.

At midnight we got up and tiptoed out the door. In my backpack I had six cheese sandwiches, a map of the Pacific Ocean, some rope, a flashlight, extra batteries, and a cell phone. It would have been nice to have a cutlass and some pistols, but it didn't matter much. I didn't know how to use them anyway.

Captain Jack had his backpack too. I could smell fish sticks in it.

We walked more than a mile through quiet streets before we saw anyone else. Then up ahead we saw Long Carla.

"Wait up," I called.

She stopped, and I heard a voice behind me say, "Yeah, wait up."

It was Sand Crab Scott and Hammerhead Jason.

When we were all together, I said, "Are we all going to the airport?"

"Arh," Hammerhead said.

"We all signed articles, didn't we?" Sand Crab said.

"'We be the crew of the good ship *Kraken*. We swears to stand together in all storms, battles, and other pirate dangers,'" Long Carla said.

"Right. So let's keep going," Captain Jack said.

By the time we got to the airport, most of the class was already there. And kids from the other classes kept coming in.

The blimp was tied to a tall post by its nose. It swung back and forth in the night breeze.

"It's big," I said.

"It's beautiful," Long Carla said.

"It's forty feet off the ground," Captain Jack said. "I wonder how Purvis plans to get into it."

A pair of headlights turned off the road and drove to where we were. Commodore Purvis got out of a taxi. He had a pair of goggles on top of his hat.

"What are you all doing here?" he shouted. "Go home. This is my adventure."

"Belay!" we all shouted. We jumped up and down and screamed, and it was just like the old days before we became pirates.

Then Long Carla blew her bosun's whistle and we all got quiet.

"Commodore Purvis, Desperate Evil Wicked Bob is everybody's captain," Long Carla said. "So pick a crew to go with you."

"I told you, there's no room!" Commodore Purvis yelled.

"Oh, yes there is," said a voice in the sky.

We all looked up. Ms. Quern's head was sticking out of a window in the little silver gondola under the blimp.

"There are seven seats in here, plus one for the pilot," she said.

"Ms. Quern, come down from there!" Commodore Purvis shouted. "That's my blimp."

"Come and get me."

"Ms. Quern, throw down the rope ladder," Commodore Purvis called up.

"Take me along or no ladder," Ms. Quern said.

"Oh, all right," Commodore Purvis said. "But no one else." Then he said "Ouch!" because Captain Jack had pecked him.

"You're taking me," Captain Jack said. "I'm his penguin."

"And I'm his nevvy," I said.

"And I'm Captain Jack's tutor," Long Carla said.

"That just leaves room for me and Hammerhead," Sand Crab said.

"But this is supposed to be my own personal adventure," Principal Purvis said.

"Forget it, Commodore. You'll never make it without us," Ms. Quern said, and all the kids roared "Arh!"

"I never get to do anything I want," Principal Purvis said. "Oh, all right, Ms. Quern. Throw down the ladder."

"First, cross your heart," Ms. Quern said.

"I cross my heart you can all go with me," Commodore Purvis said. He wasn't happy about it.

Down came the rope ladder. Up we all went. Captain Jack held on to my back with his beak and feet. The rope swayed hard as we climbed. The ground danced under me, and I didn't like it. I was glad to finally get into the gondola. It swayed too. But at least it had walls and a floor.

Commodore Purvis sat in the pilot's seat. The rest of us sat in three rows of red bus seats right behind him.

By now the sun was just coming up. I could feel the air getting hotter.

"Warm air. Just what we need," Commodore Purvis said. "Now watch this."

He pulled a lever, and the blimp let go of the mast and began to float. Two engines started, and the *Hyena of the Skies* began to move. He pulled another lever, and the blimp pointed its nose into the sky.

All the kids were waving at

us and shouting. The airfield and the town slid by underneath us. The sky was turning bright all around.

"Which way is the Pacific Ocean?" asked Commodore Purvis.

"West," we all told him.

BLIMP LESSONS

"Now, let me give you a lesson about blimps," Commodore Purvis said. "You should all know this, even though no one gets to drive it but me. First of all, it's full of helium. That's what makes it stay up. Helium is a very light gas. That big thing up there is called the envelope. It holds the helium. But inside the envelope are two more bags called ballonets. They're to hold air. By letting air in and pumping it out, I can make us go up and down. Watch this."

He turned a steering wheel that made the engines point down. Then he made them point up. The blimp's nose went in the opposite directions.

"Neat, huh?" the commodore said. "And this wheel makes us go side to side. Any questions?"

"Where is the bathroom?" said Long Carla.

"Back by the extra fuel tanks," Commodore Purvis said. "I've thought of everything."

"Where is the kitchen?" asked Ms. Quern.

"Uh-oh," said Commodore Purvis. "I didn't think of everything."

"Okay, everybody. Let's see what food we've got," Sand Crab said.

We wound up having my cheese sandwiches, Captain Jack's fish sticks, a big bag of beef jerky, some instant coffee, sixteen candy bars, four big bags of chips, two six-packs of soda, and four slices of old pizza wrapped up in foil.

"We'd better go shopping," Ms. Quern said.

"Don't be silly, Ms. Quern. You can't go shopping in the sky." Commodore Purvis laughed.

"Sooner or later we'll get to San Diego, unless you get completely lost," Ms. Quern told him. "There are lots of stores in San Diego."

We didn't get completely lost, even though we had to change course a lot to go around mountains. The blimp couldn't fly very high. We drifted over rivers and roads and lots of farms and cities. I had never traveled so far before. If this was what adventures were like, I decided I would have to go on more of them.

When we got to San Diego, we cruised low over the parking lot of a big supermarket.

"Commodore, how are we going to park this thing?" Ms. Quern said. "There's no mooring mast."

"I thought of that," Commodore Purvis said. "Just watch."

Right behind the pilot's seat there was a big metal box with a lever on it. Commodore Purvis pulled the lever, and a rattling sound came out of the box.

I ran to the window and looked out.

An anchor was dropping, dragging a long chain with it. It snagged on one of the tall lights in the parking lot, and Commodore Purvis stopped the engines.

"Now we just throw the rope ladder down," he said happily. "And when we're ready to leave, we throw the lever in the other direction. There's a motor in the box that pulls up the anchor."

"*Weighs* anchor, Commodore," Long Carla said.

"Oh. Right. That's what I meant," Commodore Purvis said.

25

The blimp bounced and tugged at the end of the chain, and the light pole creaked, but the anchor held.

"Give us some money first," Ms. Quern said.

"Oh. Money?" Commodore Purvis said. He sounded like he had never heard of it.

"We're your crew. You have to feed us," Sand Crab said.

"Oh, all right," Commodore Purvis said. He pulled out a few dollars.

"I'll peck you," Captain Jack said, and Commodore Purvis came up with a lot more.

We came back with all kinds of food that wouldn't spoil, and packed it in wherever there was room. Then we gave Commodore Purvis his change.

Sand Crab pulled up the ladder. Commodore Purvis started the engines. The anchor untangled from the lamppost. The motor in the box hauled it up, and we were on our way.

As soon as we left the market, we were over the ocean. The sun was going down and the air was cooling off, so the blimp flew lower than before. We looked out the windows at the waves, and the sun on the water. I could understand why Uncle Pirate missed the ocean, even though he was happy to live with us and was in love with Ms. Quern.

"Next stop, Hawaii," Ms. Quern said.

"Which way is that, exactly?" Commodore Purvis asked.

"Keep going west," Long Carla said slowly. "West and south."

"Would you like me to drive?" Ms. Quern asked.

"No," Commodore Purvis said. "This is still my adventure."

"How fast are we going?" Captain Jack asked.

"Oh, about sixty miles an hour," Commodore Purvis said.

Captain Jack got his notebook and pencil out of his backpack. Long Carla held the notebook for him while he wrote.

"If we fly at sixty miles an hour in a straight line to Honolulu, and Honolulu is two thousand five hundred and sixty miles from San Diego . . ." He paused. "Let's see. We're going to take forty-three and a half hours to get there. Commodore, do you plan to fly this ship all the way there?"

"Of course, it's my blimp," he said.

"Selfish," said Long Carla.

"Bad planning," Captain Jack said.

"Typical," Ms. Quern said.

"Uncle Pirate would've trained us," I said.

"Aye, aye," said Sand Crab and Hammerhead.

"I don't think so," Commodore Purvis said. "You're all too young, except Ms. Quern. Anyway, it's harder than it looks. Don't worry about me, I'll be fine."

"We're not worried about you. We're worried about us," Captain Jack said.

"Well, don't worry about you, either," Commodore Purvis said.

Ms. Quern rolled her eyes, but there was nothing much we could do. It got late, and we realized there were only two narrow beds.

"We should have brought sleeping bags," Sand Crab said.

"We can't think of everything," Hammerhead said. "We never ran away on a blimp before."

Then I had an idea.

"Uncle Pirate would make a hammock out of something," I said. And I thought I knew what he would do. Ms. Quern had not only bought groceries at the store. She had also bought secretary supplies, just in case she needed them.

"Ms. Quern, may I use your packing tape?" I said.

First, we emptied out all the paper bags. Then we

taped the bags together into long strips. Then I took the rest of the tape and hung the strips from both ends wherever there was room.

"Hammocks," I said.

"Yay, Wilson," Sand Crab and Hammerhead cheered.

"Thanks, Wilson," Long Carla said.

"Very clever," Captain Jack said.

"Good enough for now, anyway," Ms. Quern said. "When we get to Hawaii, we'll buy real ones. Won't we, Commodore?"

"Well, maybe. If there's time," Commodore Purvis said.

"Don't be cheap, Purvis, or we'll—"

I think she was going to say "mutiny," but she didn't. None of us could ever mutiny. It was in articles.

Commodore Purvis sighed.

"Oh, all right," he said. "But all this spending is spoiling my adventure."

There wasn't a TV on the blimp, but Long Carla had filled her backpack with books. She and Captain Jack took turns reading aloud *Geography of the Pacific* to us while Sand Crab played *Pirate Island* on his GameKid, and Hammerhead bounced on his seat.

There was a lot to know about the Pacific. It had the deepest this and the biggest that. One thing Captain Jack read to us got me worried. Not only was the Pacific the biggest ocean, it had the most islands. There were more than eight thousand of them. Even if we searched ten islands a day, it would take us more than eight hundred days to check them all.

"Ms. Quern, what if we can't find Uncle Pirate before the end of summer vacation?" I said. "Will we have to go back?"

"No," she said. "If the worst happens, the commodore will let you make everything up. In fact, this adventure will be extra credit. Right, Commodore?"

Commodore Purvis didn't answer.

"Uh-oh," Ms. Quern said. She got up and shook him.

"I wasn't asleep," he said. "I was studying my instruments."

"You should keep your eyes open for that," Ms. Quern said. "It works better."

"Why don't you all go to bed?" Commodore Purvis said.

So we did.

I got into my paper-bag-and-tape hammock. It crackled like it was glad to see me. The blimp swung gently back and forth, and so did we. In a minute I was fast asleep.

I woke up the next morning with the sun in my eyes.

"There's something wrong," I said. "The sun should be behind us."

I put on my glasses and looked at Commodore Purvis. His eyes were shut. He was leaning on the wheel, and we were going around and around in big, loopy circles.

"Come on, help me put him to bed," Ms. Quern said.

She and Sand Crab and Hammerhead and I put him in my hammock. Long Carla got into the pilot's seat.

"I was watching him yesterday," she said. "I can do this."

"We'll all take turns from now on," Ms. Quern said.

"I wonder how long we've been orbiting the ocean?" Sand Crab said.

"I hope we still have enough gas to get to where we're going," Hammerhead said. "Otherwise we'll have to walk."

Long Carla looked at the gas gauges.

"We have the trade winds behind us," she said. "With their help, I think we'll make it."

We all agreed to fly for one hour apiece, even Captain Jack. Then we drew straws to see who went first. I could hardly wait for my turn to fly the blimp. When it finally came, I slid into the seat and took the wheel in my hands.

It felt like that blimp had just been waiting for me. It did whatever I wanted it to. I let some air out of the ballonets and pointed the engines down, and we went up to cooler air. The blimp seemed to slide through the air, like a happy fish in a big pond.

"Wilson, you're a natural pilot," Ms. Quern said when my hour was up. "You can have my turn if you want."

"No fair!" Sand Crab and Hammerhead said.

"It's my hour, and I can do what I want with it,"

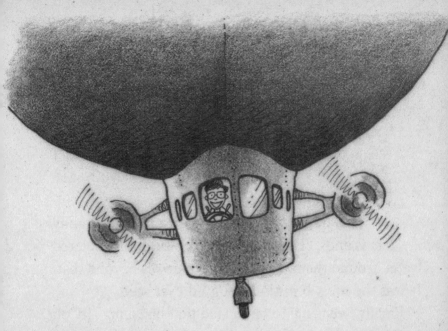

Ms. Quern said. "And don't wake up the commodore."

"Ooh. Right," Sand Crab said, and Hammerhead put his hands over his mouth and nodded his head.

When the commodore finally did wake up, it was late afternoon. First he stretched. Then he rubbed his eyes. Then he got a funny look on his face.

"Oh no! Who's flying this thing?" he shouted.

"I am," Sand Crab said. "Then it's Long Carla's turn again."

"No, no, no, no, no. This is supposed to be my adventure," Commodore Purvis said.

"You'll get a turn, just like everybody else," Ms. Quern told him. "No more falling asleep on the job. You almost got us lost."

Commodore
Purvis grumbled,
but he knew he couldn't
win an argument with Ms.
Quern. Nobody could.

Two days later we flew past a string of sandy red islands. They had rings of turquoise-colored water around them, and the deep blue sea beyond that. It was the most beautiful thing I'd ever seen.

Finally, we came to one island that had a big city on it. We flew over a beach, where a lot of people waved up at us, and found a huge mall. We anchored in the parking lot again, and went shopping.

That mall had everything. There were big ponds filled with goldfish the size of puppies, and little gardens with parrots in them. There were planters the size of small forests, and a big statue of a tiki god. We found a place that sold hammocks. Ms. Quern let us pick out whatever one we wanted. Then she made Commodore Purvis pay for them.

"This is such a bad idea," he said. "We'll only use them on this trip. Then they'll just end up in closets. Besides, those paper-bag-and-tape things Wilson made are so comfortable."

"Then you can keep one," Ms. Quern said. "But the

rest of us are getting real hammocks. Pay up."

Commodore Purvis gave the clerk a lot of money and got a little back. His face turned as white as his uniform.

"You know, we need swimsuits, too," Sand Crab said. "Just in case."

"Swimsuits? We won't have any time to go swimming," Commodore Purvis said. "Let's get back to the blimp."

"Swimsuits are a great idea," Ms. Quern said. "And then lunch."

"Lunch? When we have all this wonderful junk food

to eat?" Commodore Purvis said, and his voice shook. "Lunch would be a huge waste of time."

We all just looked at him.

"There's a swimsuit shop right over there," Long Carla said.

"Come on, Commodore," Captain Jack said. "Otherwise . . ." He pretended to peck at the Commodore's leg.

"Who ever heard of an adventure with swimsuits?" Commodore Purvis said, but he went down the mall to the swimsuit shop with all of us right behind him.

When all of us but Captain Jack and the commodore had swimsuits, we looked around for a place to eat. By now, Commodore Purvis was practically crying. "My money. My poor money," he kept saying.

"You sound awful, Commodore," Ms. Quern said. "But I'll bet some food will cheer you up."

Commodore Purvis moaned.

Close by, there was a restaurant that served about a hundred different kinds of peanut butter sandwiches. Ms. Quern made Commodore Purvis take us there for lunch. I had peanut butter and strawberry jam—my favorite. Captain Jack had peanut butter and fish.

Commodore Purvis ordered peanut butter and pickle.

"Why do you eat peanut butter and pickle, Commodore?" Sand Crab asked him.

"It's my favorite," he said. "My mother used to make them."

I didn't say anything. I was too surprised to hear that Commodore Purvis had a mother.

But Ms. Quern said, "Commodore, if there was a peanut butter and money sandwich, *that* would be your favorite."

A VERY BIG OCEAN

We left Hawaii and headed south. It wasn't long before the friendly red islands were gone, and there was nothing below us but ocean. It seemed bigger than ever.

"How far to Tahiti?" Commodore Purvis asked.

"Two thousand seven hundred and forty miles," Captain Jack said.

Ms. Quern whipped out her calculator.

"So, just under two days till we get there. Assuming we can fly sixty miles an hour the whole way and stay on course."

And we did. With seven of us flying, we each got three or four turns a day. It worked out perfectly. Commodore Purvis didn't even complain about having to share.

The first time I flew at night, I felt like there was nothing left of the world but the sky. I had a compass

to tell me where I was going, a dial to tell me how high I was, and nothing else but the sound of the engines and the light of the stars. Even though the others were asleep, I felt like I was all alone. It was a little scary.

Then I felt a beak on my shoulder and heard a sort of purring sound in my ear.

"I like it best when you fly," Captain Jack said. "The blimp feels different. Like it knows right where it's going."

"That's good, 'cause I don't," I said.

"Remember your pirate name?" Captain Jack said.

"Sure," I said. "It's Binnacle Will."

"And you remember why Captain Desperate Evil Wicked Bob called you that?"

"Because I never steers him wrong."

"Well, it's the same thing," Captain Jack said. "You're good at steering things. Good at finding your way."

"Do you think we will find Uncle Pirate?"

"We will if we look long enough."

I had a terrible thought. "What if we fly over him in the dark?"

"Well," Captain Jack said. "It's okay to fly at night now, because we know he got to Tahiti. But after we leave there, we have to stop when the sun goes down."

"I wonder if there's an anchor on board?" I said. "An anchor with a really long rope."

Captain Jack turned to me with a surprised look. I guess it was a surprised look. It's hard to tell with a penguin.

"Wilson, that's a great idea," he said.

"An anchor?" I said.

"No, a really long rope," Captain Jack said. "From now on, while we're searching, I want you to hang me under the blimp from a really long rope. I see about ten times as well as any human. If I'm down below, I'll see him, even if he's in a rowboat."

When we left Tahiti, we took off with Captain Jack spinning and swinging under us from a long rope. Hanging down along with him was a tin can on a string. That was so Captain Jack could call us if he saw anything. Someone was always waiting at our end of the string to listen.

Now that we were halfway across the Pacific, we were finally in the area where Uncle Pirate had to be. I don't know how many islands we saw. Most of them were so small that no one lived on them. A few were pretty big. Some of those had people. We asked at every one of them if they had seen any pirates, but the answer was always the same: No one had seen any.

By the end of a week we were all getting tired. It made our eyes sore to keep watching the ocean all the time. Even worse, we were beginning to realize just how hard it was going to be to find him. The ocean went on forever, and most of it was very empty.

It was hardest for Captain Jack. Being blown around by the wind was making a mess of his feathers, and his flippers got tired from flapping. When we hauled him up, he tried to joke about it.

41

"I always wanted to try flying," he said, "but I think I'd rather swim. It's cooler."

We kept searching through the bright sun-light and the huge white clouds. They were amazing. They surrounded us. Some flew alongside, and some flew overhead. Captain Jack kept disappearing into the ones below us. Then he'd pass through them and be there again, flapping at the end of his rope.

Then one afternoon, the big fluffy clouds came together and turned into a storm. A huge storm. There was thunder and lightning, and the rain was so heavy, you could hardly see the back of the blimp. We bumped and twisted through the sky, with everything in the gondola sliding and flying around the cabin.

"Whee!" Sand Crab shouted and jumped into his hammock for a ride, but after a minute he was out on the floor again, rubbing his head and moaning.

"This is very bad," I said to Hammerhead as he slid by me on the floor.

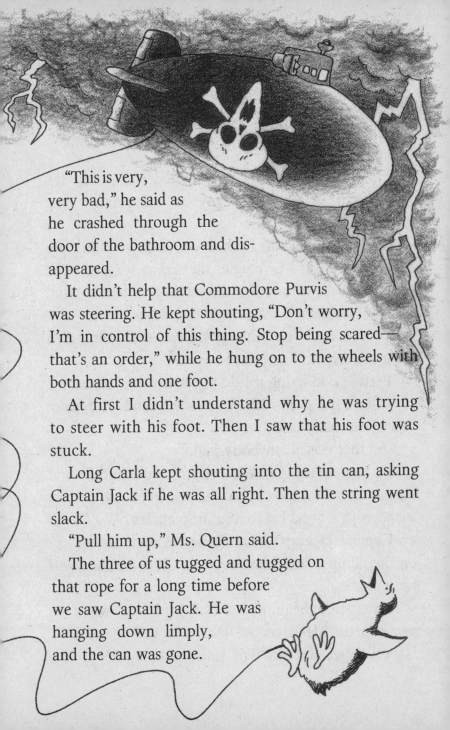

"This is very, very bad," he said as he crashed through the door of the bathroom and disappeared.

It didn't help that Commodore Purvis was steering. He kept shouting, "Don't worry, I'm in control of this thing. Stop being scared—that's an order," while he hung on to the wheels with both hands and one foot.

At first I didn't understand why he was trying to steer with his foot. Then I saw that his foot was stuck.

Long Carla kept shouting into the tin can, asking Captain Jack if he was all right. Then the string went slack.

"Pull him up," Ms. Quern said.

The three of us tugged and tugged on that rope for a long time before we saw Captain Jack. He was hanging down limply, and the can was gone.

"Oh no!" Long Carla said. "Captain Jack!"

Hammerhead Jason and Sand Crab Scott crawled over to help us, and we pulled Captain Jack into the blimp.

"Hello," he said. "Isn't this a wonderful storm? It's better than Antarctica. Fix my can thing and let me go back."

So we lowered him back down, and we didn't see him again until, like magic, the storm stopped. The sun came back, the ocean calmed down, and the wind blew softly again.

We cleaned up the gondola and untangled Commodore Purvis from the wheel.

"Pretty good flying if I do say so myself," he said.

"I liked the part with your foot," Sand Crab said. "That was really neat."

And that was all anybody said.

We kept on looking. We'd start flying at sunrise and stare at the ocean all day. At sunset, we would find an island with a good beach and drop anchor. We'd haul up Captain Jack and have dinner. Sometimes we ate on the blimp. Sometimes we went down to the island for a picnic.

It was at the beginning of our third week when we saw a small island across from a bigger one, with a lagoon between them. The sun was going down fast, so we decided to stop for the night and search the big island the next day.

It was a small island, but very pretty. The coconut palms kept dropping their nuts with soft plopping sounds. It would have been nice to have some, but they were too big and heavy. Nobody wanted to go to the trouble of getting them open. Instead we ate sandwiches and took turns tossing fish sticks to Captain Jack.

"Nice island," Commodore Purvis said. "I wonder if there's any buried treasure here." He said that at every island we came to.

"Uncle Pirate never found any buried treasure, and he looked for years," I said.

"With all due respect to the captain, he never did it scientifically," Commodore Purvis said. "I take a very different approach. I study things. I look things up. And I look at things from different angles. I ask myself questions like, 'If I were a treasure, where would pirates hide me?'"

"What sense does it make to bury treasure?" Sand Crab said. "If I had any treasure, I'd spend it."

"Me too," Hammerhead said. "I'll bet nobody ever buried treasure."

"Don't say that, don't say that," Commodore Purvis said. "Some of these islands have been visited by pirates for hundreds of years. And I'll bet that the captain's old crew were looking for treasure when they were taken prisoner."

"Aha, Purvis, I just figured it out." Captain Jack pointed a flipper at him. "You're not really interested in finding the captain. You just thought he might lead you to some pirate loot."

"Oh, wouldn't that be nice," Commodore Purvis said with a big messy smile. "I've never thought of it before. Very good, Captain Jack."

And he patted Captain Jack on the head.

"The heck you didn't think of it," Ms. Quern snarled. "That's why you didn't want us along. You don't want to share with us if the captain finds anything."

"Well, I hate sharing," Commodore Purvis said. "What's wrong with that?"

"'All treasure is to be divided up even,'" Sand Crab said. "It's in articles."

"I know, I know," Commodore Purvis said.

I remembered what had happened

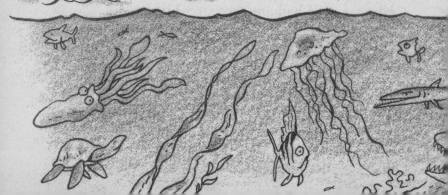

when Uncle Pirate took over our school and made everything shipshape and Bristol fashion. Commodore Purvis had seen that Uncle Pirate carried a pair of old-fashioned pistols that were worth a fortune. He tricked Uncle Pirate into giving him his guns for safekeeping, then sold them. If Ms. Quern hadn't found out what he was doing, he would have gotten away with it.

The commodore had behaved himself since then. He'd signed articles like everybody else, and he'd been a good shipmate. But I was sure he hadn't changed much. He was still Sneaky Purvis.

Captain Jack gave Commodore Purvis a cold, hard stare. Then he said, "Excuse me. I'm going to wash my head."

He waddled down to the lagoon and dived in. He swam away fast, leaving a thin line of glowing surf behind him.

We finished our dinner and cleaned up everything. We watched the sky and talked about what people were probably doing at home and how much longer it might take to find Uncle Pirate. The fire burned down.

It got late.

Captain Jack still hadn't come back.

I went down to the beach and looked across the water to the big island. It was dark

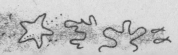

over there, except for the moonlight on the cliffs of the volcano at the middle. It was beautiful, but I wasn't in a mood to enjoy it.

I wondered if there were sharks out there and if they liked penguins.

The others climbed up into the blimp and went to bed. The lights went out in the gondola, and everything got quiet, except for the sounds of the surf and the palm trees rustling their leaves.

Finally, I saw Captain Jack coming. He was skimming through the waves in long, low jumps, coming as fast as he could.

He flung himself up on the beach, stood up, and shook himself off.

"Wilson," he said, "I found him. But I think he's in trouble."

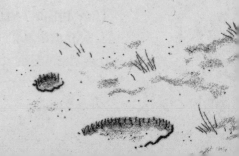

BIG BOOTS

We went back to the blimp and got everybody up.

"When I swam over to the big island, I saw a lot of footprints," Captain Jack said. "There was one set that had to be the captain. One shoe and one big, round hole that had to be his peg. There were three other sets. Big boots. All the prints went in the same direction. It looked like the big boots were chasing him."

"But where did they go?" asked Ms. Quern.

"Into a jungle," Captain Jack said. "I went that way, and after a long time I came around to the other side.

of the island. When I got there, I saw where they'd taken him."

Captain Jack fluffed up his feathers. It was a thing he did when Long Carla taught him something that he didn't understand. He kept fluffing them until whatever it was made sense to him.

"I don't know what it is, exactly," he said. "It's a huge building with a lot of smaller buildings around it. I think the smaller buildings are to live in. But I saw a lot of people going in and out of the huge one. Some of them had big boots on. They were the ones with guns and sticks. Then there were others with no boots. They were carrying big boxes out of the building and taking

them down to a ship. And a lot of them were dressed like pirates."

"Where was Uncle Pirate?" I asked.

"He was with the ones without boots," Captain Jack said. "The ones with the boots were making him carry two boxes instead of one. I think they were punishing him."

"We've got to go get him now!" Sand Crab said.

"Let's go get all of them!" Hammerhead said.

"Not so fast," Long Carla said. "If we go running around in a jungle at night, we could get lost in two minutes."

"I agree," Commodore Purvis said. "Besides, if those

pirates are working that hard, they need their rest. Tomorrow will be plenty of time."

"Oh, Commodore," Ms. Quern said. "Trust you to find the worst reason for doing the right thing."

The next morning we all woke up early. All but Sand Crab and Hammerhead. They were already gone. They had left us a note.

> Gone to rescue the captain.
> Back 4 lunch.
> Hammerhead and Sand crab
> P.S. We took the candy bars
> for emergencies.

We waited until lunchtime, but no one came back. No one came at one o'clock, or at two.

"We'd better go after them," Long Carla said at last.

"We can't," Commodore Purvis said. "We don't even know how they got across the lagoon."

"They swam, of course," Captain Jack said. "They can't fly, you know."

"Oh, of course," Commodore Purvis said. "Well, I can't swim."

"Good. Then you can stay here and guard the blimp," Ms. Quern said.

"That is a good idea," Commodore Purvis said. "Just let me know when you want me to do anything."

Ms. Quern snorted. "Come on, mates. Let's get going."

We all put on our swimsuits and dived into the ocean. All but Captain Jack, who didn't need one, and Commodore Purvis, who stood on the beach and waved good-bye.

Swimming in the ocean was very different from swimming in a pool, but the water was warm and the waves inside the lagoon were small. We made it across with no trouble.

Ms. Quern had even brought along a plastic sack with T-shirts and shoes for each of us, except Captain Jack, tied up inside. I had been almost as smart. I had put my Swiss Army knife and my glasses in a small plastic bag, and stuffed it in my suit.

The footprints Hammerhead and Sand Crab left went straight toward the jungle. We followed them into a thick forest of funny-looking trees and long vines. Then we followed Captain Jack. First him, then me, then Long Carla, then Ms. Quern.

It got dark early under the trees. It was like night in there, even before the sun went down. But Captain Jack kept walking, slow and steady.

"How can you even see in this?" I asked him.

"If I can find my way around Antarctica during a six-month night, a little jungle twilight isn't going to be a problem," he said. "Besides"—he bent over and picked up a candy wrapper—"Sand Crab and Hammerhead left us a trail."

We went a little farther and saw a yellow glow through the trees.

"Careful now," Captain Jack whispered. "Those guys with the big boots may be around."

He threw himself down and slid forward on his

stomach, quiet as a shadow. We followed him as well as we could.

At the edge of the jungle we could see the huge building and the little ones that looked like cabins. There was a barbed-wire fence around the whole thing, and bright lights that lit up every corner. The guys with big boots were everywhere.

"Look at that," Ms. Quern said.

There, pulled up on the beach, was the *Hyena of the Seas*, Uncle Pirate's old ship. I had heard Uncle Pirate tell so many stories about it, I recognized it at once. It looked sad, like it missed the ocean. But everything was there. Masts, sails, and even the old-fashioned cannons sticking out of its sides.

Out by the dock was a much bigger ship. Its cranes were unloading containers the size of boxcars. When the last one had thumped down, a line of pirates came marching out of the huge building and down to the dock. The guys with big boots were on both sides of them, keeping them in line.

"Look," Ms. Quern whispered.

At the head of the line was Uncle Pirate. At the back were Sand Crab and Hammerhead.

When they reached the dock, the pirates opened the big containers and dragged everything out of them and back into the huge building. Then they loaded the boxes that were waiting on the dock into the containers. It took a long time. When they were finally finished, they looked very tired.

The guys in big boots pushed them back into line and sent them marching back into the big building.

Then the ship started its engines and backed away from the dock. We watched its lights get smaller and smaller as it sailed away. At last, it looked like stars moving against the night.

"Pretty," Long Carla said.

"But up to no good," Ms. Quern said.

"What's going on?" I asked. "Are they in some kind of prison?"

"What kind of prison has ships coming and going?" Captain Jack said. "Besides, they wouldn't put Sand Crab and Hammerhead in prison for no reason."

"We need to get someone inside," Ms. Quern said. "Me."

"Why would they let you in?" Long Carla asked.

"Because whatever kind of place that is, they'll have secretaries," Ms. Quern said. "All I need to do is walk up there. I'll bet they'll give me an interview. I'll find out what they're doing."

"But Ms. Quern," I said. "You're not dressed for work."

"Good point," she said. "Okay,

I'll swim back to the blimp tomorrow and get my dress. Then I'll go and apply for a job."

This did not sound like a good idea, but nobody could think of a better one.

We decided we might as well sleep.

But I didn't sleep very well. I didn't like Ms. Quern's idea. I was sure she was so much in love with Uncle Pirate that she wasn't thinking straight. Whoever had made prisoners of the pirates, Sand Crab, and Hammerhead would do the same to her.

Finally, I got up. I decided to go for a swim out to that dock. I was sure I could find out something from there. "After all," I said to myself, "Uncle Pirate's *my* uncle."

I tiptoed down to the water and slid in. When I reached the dock, I hid under it and moved as close as I could to the beach. It gave me a perfect view of the front of the huge building. It didn't look like a

bad place. It had two big doors that slid open and a black road leading to them from the dock. The only other thing to see was a flag. It was a flag I recognized. Anybody would have. It was famous all over the world. It was white, with a winged tennis shoe on it, and a blue shape that everyone called the Swish. MERCURY SNEAKERS was printed on the flag in black letters.

"A sneaker factory?" I said. "Why would they put a sneaker factory here?"

Then I had another idea.

I got out of the water and dried myself off as well as I could.

Then I walked up to the front of the big building and knocked.

No one came to the door, so I knocked again. I kept on knocking until one of the guys in big boots came around the side of the building. He was a tall man, bigger than Uncle Pirate, and, even in the middle of the night, he was wearing sunglasses. He did not look friendly.

"Hello," I said. "I'm here to buy shoes. How much for a pair of Wingtip Wonders?"

A RIGHT LOST CREW

The guy in sunglasses called three other guys, and they surrounded me. They took me around the side of the building to a little door and unlocked it.

Inside, the building was full of machines. The smell of hot rubber was everywhere. I saw long lines of sewing machines stitching one shoe after another. Big bolts of cloth were being cut into patterns by blades that were sharper than cutlasses. And at every one of them, there was at least one pirate. They all looked miserable.

The four guards marched me over to a metal staircase. Up at the top was a room with windows that looked out over the factory floor.

The first guard knocked on the door.

"We got another one, Mr. Purvis," he said.

There was a man sitting at a huge desk. A nameplate on it said PRESIDENT PRENTISS PURVIS. The man behind the desk looked like he could have been Commodore Purvis's brother.

It was a nice office. There was a lot of expensive furniture, and a thick carpet. On the back wall was a life-size oil painting of President Purvis dressed like the god Mercury. Except that instead of winged sandals, he was wearing a pair of Wingtip Wonders.

There was only one other picture on the walls: a little gray photograph of Commodore Purvis. He was young and smiling and had all his hair. Just above the picture were big black letters that spelled out HATE.

I decided not to mention that I knew the commodore.

"These pirates are getting smaller," President Purvis said. "You're the shortest one yet."

"Oh, I'm not a pirate," I said. "I just came to buy shoes."

"You look just like the last two pirates we caught," President Purvis said. "Small. Young. Wearing a bathing suit. I'll bet you have a name like Sand Crab or Hammerhead. Haven't you?"

"No really, I just want some sneakers," I said.

"How many pairs?" President Purvis asked.

"Just one," I said.

"One?" President Purvis said. "One pair isn't enough. You need lots and lots of sneakers. You need sneakers for walking, sneakers for running, sneakers for playing sports, sneakers for not playing sports, sneakers for watching television, sneakers for video games, sneakers for reading . . ." He got up and came over to me. "The average person needs at least one hundred and eighteen pairs of sneakers to be happy," he said. "And you only want one. Therefore, you are not happy. Are you?"

President Purvis looked angry with me for wanting only one pair of sneakers. I thought he might be crazy.

"I'm not real happy right now," I said. "But I don't think sneakers have much to do with it."

President Purvis took off his glasses and stared at me hard. "How were you planning to pay for your sneakers? We accept all major credit cards," he said.

I was getting scared. And I figured I had found out all I could about this place.

"Maybe I'd better go," I said. "It's getting late."

"Not so fast," President Purvis said. "It's never too late to buy sneakers."

"Oh, never mind," I said. "I'll come back sometime when I can afford a hundred and eighteen pairs."

"I'll bet you can afford something," President Purvis said. "Turn out your pockets. I want to know how much money you have."

"I'm wearing a bathing suit," I said. "I don't have any pockets."

"No pockets?" President Purvis said. "No pockets means no money. No money means no sneakers. No sneakers means you are lying to me. Why did you really come, pirate?"

The guards moved to stand beside me.

I was really scared now.

"I'm not a pirate," I said. "I've never even signed articles."

"Never signed articles, eh?" President Purvis shouted. "How do you know what articles are if you're not a pirate? I knew it. You came to steal my shoes."

"I'm not a pirate, I'm a boy," I said. "Let me go."

"You are a pirate," said President Purvis. "And we know just what to do with pirates, don't we men? Put him on the day shift."

"Yes, sir, Mr. Purvis," the guards said.

They took me out of the office, down the stairs, out of the factory, and over to a cabin that had bars on the windows.

"We'll have to throw you in with the old guy," one of the guards said. "We're full up. Pirates everywhere."

He unlocked two locks.

Another guard banged on the door.

"Belay!" said a voice I knew.

"Hey, old-timer, open up," the guard said.

The door cracked open, and they shoved me in.

"Who be this bilge rat?" said Uncle Pirate.

He looked at me like he'd never seen me before. I looked at him the same way.

"Just another kid," the guard said. "Bring him to work with you tomorrow."

"Ye'll not make a lubberly babyminder out of Desperate Evil Wicked Bob," Uncle Pirate said.

"Whatever." The guard laughed. "See you tomorrow."

"Ye're not fit to chop for chum!" Uncle Pirate shouted.

Then he slammed the door. As soon as it was closed, he grabbed me and held me so tightly, I could hardly breathe.

"Nevvy!" said Uncle Pirate. "Nevvy!"

We had to catch each other up. When I was done, Uncle Pirate told his story.

"I made sail from Tahiti in as fine a trim little outrigger as ever caught the west wind," Uncle Pirate said.

"The dolphins kept me company, and they be good luck, you know. But the day came when there weren't no dolphins, and sure enough a mighty typhoon come up and swamped me. I got me craft bailed out, all right, but my mast was shivered, and my compass and charts was lost. I didn't know one bit of coral from another.

"'Desperate Evil Wicked Bob,' I says to myself, 'it looks like ye'll never see Ferocious Lovely Eunice nor Nevvy nor Captain Jack nor any of the fine young pirates back at home again.'

"But then a dolphin come back. Just one, but a real decent fellow. I followed him best as I could, paddling the outrigger along. We passed one island and another, and I found water on one, and bananas on another, and so I kept on, following the dolphin.

"Finally, I sees a mountaintop and steers for it. And I comes upon this place. And I sees the old *Hyena of the Seas* beached and looking all forlorn. And I stops and I asks the first swab I meets, 'Where be my crew?' And he brings me here, and before you can touch fuse to a twenty-four pounder,

they has me locked up along with my old shipmates.

"But now, Nevvy, ye be here," Uncle Pirate said. "Me old crew been waitin'. I told 'em all, secretlike, 'My nevvy's coming. And when he gets here, he'll bring the crew that'll rescue the whole sorry cargo, and sail ye to charted waters.' And here ye be. That Purvis and his big-booted bilge rats don't know what they're in for."

The door opened again, and the guards threw Hammerhead and Sand Crab into the room. It was really crowded now.

"Caught 'em tryin' to escape," one guard said.

The door slammed.

"Dang," Hammerhead said. "Now we have to make sneakers again tomorrow."

"Wilson, you've got to get us out of here," Sand Crab said. "Making sneakers is bilgewater."

I was not understanding this at all.

"But, Uncle Pirate," I said, "why do they keep you here making sneakers? Why don't they just hire people to do it?"

"That Purvis be too cheap to pay anyone decent wages," Uncle Pirate said. "The first workers he brung in all ran away the first chance they got. Then he tried little kids and paid them even less. But some of them had been to school. They knowed where they was and figured out how to get home. They all escaped together. Then the *Hyena of the Seas* showed up, looking for plunder. Well, it wasn't no trick at all to make them swab jockeys who marooned me come ashore. Purvis promised them a party and told them he knew where treasure was hid. And the poor fools has been here ever since, making sneakers."

Uncle Pirate shook his head. "Pirates be stupid as a shelf of clams, when you get down to it."

"But now Wilson's here. He'll think up a plan," Sand Crab said.

"Arh," Uncle Pirate said. "A most terrible plan, Nevvy. That be what we want."

"Why me?" I said.

"You're the smartest one," Hammerhead said.

"I am?" I said.

"Sure," Sand Crab said. "Hammerhead and I are fighters, not thinkers."

"And I got caught when I tried to lead a mutiny," Uncle Pirate said. "That be why they locks me up at night now."

"So it's your turn," Sand Crab said.

"Arh," Uncle Pirate said. "So, Nevvy, what be your plan?"

"I'll get started on it," I said.

We all lay down on Uncle Pirate's one blanket.
"Okay," I said. "I'll think of a plan."

I stayed awake a long time, but I couldn't think of
a thing.

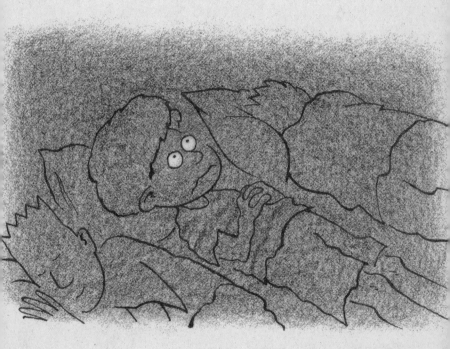

A MOST TERRIBLE PLAN

The next morning the guards got us all up for breakfast. We ate in a cafeteria. We all got the same thing, and it tasted worse than the food at Very Elementary.

"What *is* this stuff?" I asked Uncle Pirate.

"Eggplant," Uncle Pirate said. "It be all we ever gets."

"Aye," the pirate on the other side of me said. "They say Purvis owns an eggplant ranch somewheres."

"I likes it," said a pirate close by. "It be better than I could ever do. Can I have yours if ye don't want it?"

"Binnacle Will, meet Rotten Ralph, what was cook on the old *Hyena of the Seas*," Uncle Pirate said. "Rotten, this be Binnacle Will. And Binnacle, that lubber on the other side of ye be

Contemptible Charlie, me old master gunner."

Uncle Pirate whispered in a foghorn voice, "Binnacle Will be my nevvy. Didn't I tell ye he'd come?"

All around the table, the pirates were buzzing the word "nevvy." One or two of them ducked their heads.

"My nevvy will craft us a most terrible plan," Uncle Pirate said.

"We be ready to take yer orders, Binnacle, just as soon as ye gives the word," said the pirate sitting across from me. Then he sniffled. Then he started to cry.

I patted his hand. "There, there," I said.

"Oh, it be nothing," the pirate said. "I just cries when I gets excited. It be why they calls me Disgusting Earl. But I be fierce, Binnacle. Ask the captain."

"Fierce and ruthless," Uncle Pirate said happily.

"Hey, just a minute. You're the one who marooned my uncle," I said.

"Aye," Disgusting Earl said. "I broke me articles. We all did. And look how we ended up. We means to be faithful shipmates now. We sees the need of it. And so I says—we all says—just give the word."

But what word was I supposed to give? I still didn't have an idea. I didn't even have an idea for an idea.

When we had all finished our eggplant, the big boots marched us over to the factory.

They put me with Sand Crab and Hammerhead making the rubber for the sneaker soles.

"Hey, Binnacle," Hammerhead said. "Got the plan yet?"

"Still working on it," I said.

But making sneakers did not help my thinking. Big pots of hot white rubber steamed and bubbled and blooped. In just a few minutes I was so thirsty I could have drunk a whole case of anything. It was hard to think about anything else.

I did come up with one plan. It would have worked, too. But it needed a tank. And then I came up with another, but it needed me to be invisible.

The morning went by. Then we got lunch, which was so bad that even Rotten Ralph didn't like it.

"Has ye got the plan yet, Binnacle?" Disgusting Earl whispered. "This be the worst eggplant yet."

Everyone was looking at me. Disgusting Earl was starting to cry. I said the first thing that came into my head.

"Wait till I shout, 'Bongo, bongo, bongo.' Then go for the guards."

"Bongo, bongo, bongo." The whisper ran around the tables. The pirates grinned at one another.

Now all I needed was a plan to go with the words.

We went back to work. Making sneakers was the most boring thing I'd ever done. I felt really sorry for the pirates who'd been doing it for months. Making a big vat of rubber boiling hot, then pouring it into molds wasn't just boring, though. It turned out to be dangerous.

I was very tired from the day before, and last night I had stayed awake trying to figure out how to escape. And lunch made me sleepier. So sleepy that my eyes closed without my telling them to, and I almost fell into the vat of bubbling hot rubber.

Sand Crab grabbed my arm.

"Be careful, Binnacle," he said. "You could end up a rubber ball."

That sounded awful. I saw myself bouncing across the floor, bumping Disgusting Earl off his seat. Making him cry. And then I saw my plan. I didn't know if it was a most terrible plan or not. But I was sure it would work. Almost sure. At least it didn't need a tank.

I told Hammerhead and Sand Crab.

"Look, there aren't that many guards," I said. "I've been counting. There are a lot more pirates, but the guards have the clubs and guns. But I'll bet they won't do anything if we've got President Purvis. So all we have to do is get Purvis."

"Great idea," Hammerhead said. "Only how are we supposed to do it?"

"Simple," I said. "You two sneak off and hide someplace close to the stairs to his office. Then I start shouting that you've both fallen into the rubber. I'll bet all the guards will come over to see what's happening. That's when you run up the stairs and jump Purvis. If that works, I shout, 'Bongo, bongo, bongo.'"

"You want us to beat up President Purvis?" Sand Crab asked. His eyes were shining.

"I get dibs on biting his ears off," Hammerhead said.

"Let's go," Sand Crab said. "Give us five minutes, Binnacle. Then start shouting."

I didn't have a watch, so I started counting— "Thousand one, thousand two, thousand three"—until I got to sixty. Then I started over.

I was so happy thinking that in just a little while we'd all be free. We'd drag the *Hyena of the Seas* back into the water. We'd hoist sail, and Long Carla and Uncle Pirate would chart a course for home.

"Thousand fifty-eight, thousand fifty-nine, thousand sixty. Three," I whispered.

Two more minutes.

Then the doors of the factory slid open. Two guards walked in with someone short between them, and I lost count.

One of the guards signaled for the machines to be shut down.

"Hey, you guys, listen to this," he said.

And Captain Jack said, "Excuse me, gentlemen. Can any of you help me find my iceberg? I need to get to Antarctica."

"He's got an iceberg?" a guard asked.

"It was right down on the beach," Captain Jack said. "But now I can't find it."

"Well, let's go take a look," another guard said.

"If I can just get back to Antarctica, everything will be fine," Captain Jack said. "I'm needed there. I'm the president, you see."

"There's no such thing as a president of Antarctica," said the biggest guard.

"And I suppose there's no such thing as a talking penguin, either," Captain Jack said.

"Good point," said the guard.

"Please help me find my iceberg," Captain Jack went on. "I must get back home before it melts."

"We make sneakers here," the second guard said. "We don't have time to search for icebergs."

"Oh, sneakers?" said Captain Jack. "There is a huge market for sneakers in Antarctica. All of us penguins, going around barefoot. If you help me find my iceberg, I could see you get the contract."

"That's different," said the biggest guard. "Come on, you guys."

All of the guards went outside, herding the pirates with them. I went too.

The beach was empty.

"No icebergs around here," the first guard said.

"My mistake," said Captain Jack. "It's up there."

He pointed his beak in the air.

There, just overhead, was the *Hyena of the Skies.*

"That's no iceberg," one of the guards said.

The door to the gondola opened, and Ms. Quern stood there with a rope around her waist. She had a big bag in front of her. As the blimp passed overhead, she dumped it out.

Coconuts were falling out of the sky.

"Coconuts?" the biggest guard said. "Who's afraid of—"

Then one hit him right on the head, and he fell on the sand.

Just then, the guns on the *Hyena of the Seas* all fired at once. The air shook. Smoke rose high over the masts, and the wall of the factory crumbled.

"Oh no!" I said.

Sand Crab and Hammerhead were still in there.

The blimp turned around and swooped even lower. I saw more coconuts fall from the gondola.

The guards just stood there, looking. So did the pirates. Nobody knew what to do next.

Except me, Binnacle Will.

"Bongo, bongo, bongo!" I shouted.

I picked up a coconut and threw it at a guard. It bounced off his head.

Captain Jack, who was still being held between two guards, started pecking right and left.

"Board, ye lubbers! Board! Follow me!" Uncle Pirate shouted. "Follow me, Nevvy! Bongo, bongo, bongo!"

And that was all it took. Pirates may not be smart,

but they sure can fight. Especially when you give them some coconuts. In a few minutes the guards were all knocked out or made prisoners. The pirates had taken their guns and clubs.

The *Hyena of the Skies* passed slowly overhead. The rope ladder fell over the side, and Ms. Quern climbed down.

"Me secretary!" Uncle Pirate shouted. "Me ferocious, lovely secretary."

"Arh, Captain!" Ms. Quern shouted back.

Then out of the ruined factory ran President Purvis. Hammerhead and Sand Crab were right behind him.

"Help, help!" President Purvis yelled. "I'm being beaten up. Save me."

But there was no one to save him, and Sand Crab and Hammerhead chased him up and down the beach until they caught him and pounded him just the way they used to beat me up back home.

We saw the skull and crossbones go up on the *Hyena of the Seas*. Long Carla waved from the deck.

Every pirate who had a hat on

took it off. Every pirate cheered.

Ms. Quern jumped down onto the sand.

Then the blimp flew over to the ship, and Long Carla tied its black nose to the mainmast. It hung over the ship like a huge flag. All the pirates cheered.

Commodore Purvis climbed down the rope ladder to the deck of the ship. He walked over to us with Long Carla beside him.

"That was fun, dropping those coconuts," Commodore Purvis said. "And I wasn't a bit scared."

"Captain Jack tricked the guards into coming outside where I could get at them and bringing you guys along," Ms. Quern said. "Otherwise Long Carla couldn't have fired the guns."

Sand Crab and Hammerhead finished beating up President Purvis and dragged him over to us.

"Those cannons were great," Sand Crab said. "Purvis had locked himself in his office. But when his factory started to collapse, he unlocked it and ran. That's when we got him."

The pirates were dancing on the sand, and bashing the guards with coconuts just for fun. Disgusting Earl was crying, of course. He picked up the commodore and swung him around and around.

"Ye be the fiercest old dogfish ever sailed the skies," he roared. "Whoever ye be, I calls ye shipmate."

"Thank you very much," Commodore Purvis said. "Please put me down."

Then he saw President Purvis.

"Oh, ho," the commodore said. "In fact, yo-ho-ho, and a bottle of rum. What are you doing here, my rotten, no-good big brother?"

"Get off my island, you little creep," President Purvis yelled.

"You can't scare me anymore. I'm a pirate," said Commodore Purvis, and he threw a coconut at his brother. "Bonk," he said when it hit.

"Make him stop doing that," President Purvis complained. "It's not fair."

"Oh, it's fair ye want, is it?" Uncle Pirate said. "Well, ye shall have all the fairness ye can handle. I calls masthead."

MASTHEAD

Masthead was punishment.

First, Uncle Pirate made President Purvis and his guards drag the *Hyena of the Seas* down to the water. That was very hard work. They were all worn out by the time the ship was floating again.

But Uncle Pirate wasn't finished.

"There be sea worms eating the hull of my ship that I likes better than ye," Uncle Pirate told the guards. "Ye deserves a horrible fate."

"Make 'em make sneakers," Disgusting Earl said.

"For no pay," Contemptible Charlie said.

"That be fair," Uncle Pirate said. "But then we'd be havin' to stay here to keep 'em at it. 'Twould be best to maroon them."

"But Captain, ships stops here all the time to get shoes," Contemptible Charlie said.

"Let's send out a message that the factory has shut down," Ms. Quern said. "On the Internet. Then nobody will come here anymore."

"What be an Internet?" Disgusting Earl asked.

"A thing secretaries knows all about," Uncle Pirate said. "Aye, Ferocious Lovely Eunice. Send out that message. Then make ready to hoist sail."

"As for ye, Prisoner President Purvis, ye be the lowest, lousiest, no-good bucket of swill I ever clapped eye on. I can't think of anything bad enough to do to ye.

But fortunately I has a man here who can. Commodore Purvis, what shall we do with this brother of yours?"

President Purvis spoke up.

"Putnam, I'm rich. If you help me, I'll give you all my money."

"All of it?" Commodore Purvis asked.

"Yes, all of it," President Purvis said.

Commodore Purvis smiled. It was the worst smile

I'd ever seen.

"I promise," he said, "I'll take you with me on my blimp when I go."

Commodore Purvis was going to be rich at last.

"Finally," he said. "After reading all those books about getting rich and coming all the way out here to rescue all of you, I have my reward. Oh, it's good. I'm good. I'm so good."

All the pirates growled at him.

"You're forgetting something, Commodore," Ms. Quern told him.

"I am? What?" Commodore Purvis said.

"You're forgetting that if you don't share with us, we're going to leave you here with your brother," she said.

"Well, of course I'm going to share," Commodore Purvis said. "I was just coming to that part."

"Oh, good," Ms. Quern said.

So we spent the next couple of hours figuring out just how much money President Purvis had and dividing it up according to articles. We all got a lot. Commodore Purvis wasn't exactly rich anymore, but at least he didn't have to be marooned on the island.

By now the sun was getting low.

"Captain, the tide be turning," Disgusting Earl said. "Mayhap this be a good time to hoist anchor."

"Hoist anchor, Disgusting Earl?" Uncle Pirate said. "For what port?"

"For whatever port you says, Captain. You be our captain again, if ye'll take us back. Aye, mates?"

"Aye, aye!" all the pirates shouted.

"We be ready to board and burn, pillage, and plunder

wherever you says," Contemptible Charlie said.

"For whatever port I says?" said Uncle Pirate. "Do ye all swear it?"

"We swears by Davy Jones," they all said.

"And yet ye could not find yer way from this beach without me other crew," Uncle Pirate said. "It were not guards and fences kept ye here, ye sardine heads. It were yer own ignorance. Ye had to be rescued by a few of me new shipmates, as had been to school and done their homework. And a penguin and a secretary."

"And me," said Commodore Purvis.

"Aye, and even a Purvis," Uncle Pirate said. "And now ye be rescued, ye might as well still be marooned. Ye be a sad and sorry lot, and I am not minded to be captain over ye."

"Please, Captain," Disgusting Earl said. "Don't put us ashore."

Then all the pirates started to yell that they'd be good shipmates and never cause trouble, but Uncle Pirate just stood there with his arms crossed.

Then a high, loud whistle cut through their noise, and everyone stopped talking.

Long Carla took the bosun's whistle out of her mouth.

"Captain, I can chart a course if you want," she said.

She had her book on the Pacific under her arm.

"Proceed, Long Carla," Uncle Pirate said.

Long Carla looked through the book until she found the map she wanted.

"We're right about here," she said.

"And how shall we sail these vast and mighty waters?" Uncle Pirate said.

"Well, it won't be as easy as it was getting here," she said. "The winds are going to be against us a lot of the time. But if we just keep heading northeast, we'll get back to America sooner or later."

"Ye see, ye scurvy sons of sea cooks?" Uncle Pirate

said. "That be what ye should all be able to do. And that be why ye must all come back with me and go to school."

"Nay, Captain!" the pirates shouted. "No school!"

But Uncle Pirate said, "I has yer oaths by Davy Jones."

"Please, Captain," Disgusting Earl said. "We all hated school. That be why we ran away and became pirates. Don't make us go back."

Uncle Pirate shook his head.

"Ye must all come back with us, and ye must all attend classes. I'll have no more ignorant blowfish for shipmates. But one thing I'll promise ye: Ye shall each have one of me new crew to help ye learn."

"We won't do no homework," Contemptible Charlie said. "We hates homework."

"Then ye can rot here with these lubberly guards," Uncle Pirate said.

Hammerhead walked over to Contemptible Charlie and took his hand.

"It's okay," he said. "I hate homework too. But you get used to it."

"Ye hates it, but ye does it?" Contemptible Charlie said.

"Arh," Hammerhead said.

"Mayhap it wouldn't be so hard if we was to do it together," Contemptible Charlie said.

"I'll help you with yours if you want," Sand Crab said to Disgusting Earl.

"Thankee, shipmate," Disgusting Earl said.

"Now let's be hoisting sail for home," Uncle Pirate said.

"Isn't anybody going to go with me?" Commodore Purvis said.

"I will," Sand Crab said.

"Me too," Hammerhead said.

"And Disgusting Earl and Contemptible Charlie must

go with ye," Uncle Pirate said. "There, Commodore, ye has your crew."

The rest of us walked down the pier to the *Hyena of the Seas*. We raised her anchor and hoisted her sails. Uncle Pirate took the wheel and steered her northeast, with Long Carla beside him. Ms. Quern was walking up and down the deck, making sure everything was shipshape and Bristol fashion. Captain Jack swam beside us, flying through the waves.

I stood at the bow, watching the beautiful sunset. Just above us the *Hyena of the Skies* was glistening in

the glowing air. I could hear the sound of her engines. Everything was shipshape and Bristol fashion.

Then, out of the gondola, fell a man tied to a rope. It was President Purvis. He was swinging and swaying, just like Captain Jack had done, but he didn't seem to be liking it. We could hear him crying for help.

"Oh well," I said. "At least the commodore's keeping his promise."

"Arh," Uncle Pirate said. "And that be a first for a Purvis."

Rotten Ralph climbed up on the poop deck beside us. He was wearing a wonderful hat that he'd left on the ship when the big boots took him prisoner. Now he waved it over his head and shouted, "Three cheers for Captain Desperate Evil Wicked Bob! Hip, hip—"

But Uncle Pirate held up his hand.

"Nay, you bilge buckets," he said. "It weren't me as did it. If it were me, we'd all still be in yon hulk, turning out Soft Top Slinkers and such. It were all

them as saved us. Three cheers for Nevvy."

"But, Uncle Pirate," I said. "We all rescued each other. You and me and Ms. Quern and Captain Jack and Long Carla and Hammerhead and Sand Crab and Commodore Purvis. And even you pirates fought like—well, like very tough guys."

"Arhhh!" the pirates agreed.

"All right, then. Three cheers for everybody," Uncle Pirate said.

We all cheered three times for ourselves and for each other. But I cheered for the one who'd brought us together and made us a crew. I cheered for Uncle Pirate.

GLOSSARY

Articles: The contract signed by a pirate.

Ballonet: A bag inside the envelope of a blimp for holding air. Since air is heavier than the helium inside the blimp, filling the ballonet or emptying it helps the blimp to maneuver up and down.

Belay: To tie up a rope's end by winding it around something. Or, to stop doing something.

Bilge: The space between the lowest deck and the bottom of the ship. Dark, wet, and very smelly.

Binnacle: The box where the ship's compass is kept.

Bosun: Really spelled *boatswain*, but never pronounced that way. In charge of the deck crew and the crews of any small boats.

Bristol fashion: Neat, clean, well-organized.

Chum: Chopped-up fish parts thrown overboard to attract other fish.

Commodore: The rank above captain. A commander of two or more ships. Sometimes it is used as a courtesy title.

Gondola: The passenger compartment on a blimp.

Helium: The second lightest gas. Used in balloons instead of hydrogen, which is even lighter, because helium will not explode.

Lubber: A clumsy, stupid person. Not a good shipmate.

Masthead: Captain's court aboard ship.

Mollymockery: The rowdy behavior of drunken sailors on Greenland whaling ships.

Poop deck: The highest deck at the stern of a sailing ship.